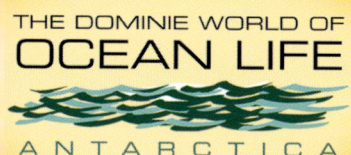

THE DOMINIE WORLD OF
OCEAN LIFE

ANTARCTICA

Ocean Travelers

WRITTEN & PHOTOGRAPHED
BY KIM WESTERSKOV, Ph.D.

1. Seabirds 2
2. Albatrosses 5
3. Penguins 7
4. Baleen Whales 10
5. Toothed Whales 14
6. Dolphins and Porpoises 17
7. Seals and Sea Lions 19
8. Fish 21
9. Fast Fish 24
10. The Drifters 26
11. Turtles and Squid 29
    Glossary 32
    Index .... Inside back cover

Dominie Press, Inc.

1
Seabirds

The open sea is a challenging place for birds to live. There is no shelter from violent storms or from the burning sun. Only about 300 **species** of birds have adapted to this challenging **habitat**—not many of the nearly 10,000 species on our planet. These birds spend most of their lives at sea, often coming ashore only to lay eggs and rear their young.

Some seabirds, such as gulls and pelicans, do not fly far from land, while others may not see land for months, or even years, at a time. The seabirds that have best adapted to the open ocean are the **tubenoses**, which include the large albatrosses and the smaller petrels and shearwaters. They get their name from the tube-shaped nostrils on top of their beaks.

Gannets are large, colorful seabirds. They catch fish by diving into the sea with their wings folded neatly behind them. Once they are underwater, they can use their wings to chase their prey, sometimes as deep as seventy feet. ▶

▲ *A seagull takes a look underwater.*

Birds of the open ocean do not need fresh water. They are able to either drink salt water or get enough water from their food. But too much salt kills birds, so special glands in their head remove the salt, which runs out of their nostrils and back into the sea.

Many seabirds make long journeys between their feeding grounds and their breeding grounds. The champion traveler is the Arctic tern, which **migrates** from the **Arctic** to **Antarctica** and back again every year—a round trip of 25,000 miles. This is the longest journey made by any animal on Earth. In its lifetime, this slender bird flies a distance that is equivalent to a return trip to the moon.

2

Albatrosses

Albatrosses are remarkable birds. They spend their lives soaring over wild, stormy seas. Using a technique called dynamic soaring, they can ride the wind and updrafts from the waves for hours without a single flap of their long wings. Their wingspan can measure up to about eleven feet. If the winds are right, albatrosses can fly more than 1,000 miles in a single day. They land on the water only to eat, or when there is no wind.

▲ *A royal albatross pair rests in their nest. Albatrosses spend their first three or more years entirely at sea, riding the winds and resting on the water. Not until they are four to six years old do they return to visit the island where they were born. Albatrosses need land only to nest and raise their young.*

Albatrosses feed on squid, fish, and **krill** from the sea, and they will dive after it if they need to. The largest albatrosses can dive just a few feet, but the smaller sooty albatrosses can reach depths of forty feet.

Albatrosses come ashore only to nest and raise their young, usually on small, windswept islands far from any humans. They are amazing navigators. After spending their first three or more years at sea, albatrosses find their way back to the island where they were born. If they aren't accidentally killed, albatrosses live longer than most other birds. They normally reach thirty to forty years of age, and a few may live to be eighty!

▼ *A wandering albatross glides gracefully over the waves. The royal and wandering albatross have the longest wings of any bird in the world.*

3
Penguins

Penguins are birds, even though they don't look much like birds. On land they walk upright like people. And they cannot fly, although they are excellent swimmers. Even their feathers, which cover most of their bodies, look more like scales than feathers. No wonder the early explorers didn't know what kind of animal they were!

All penguins live in the southern hemisphere, and most live in cold waters. Penguins have made many

▲ *Getting into the water is always a dangerous time for penguins, especially Adèlie penguins. A leopard seal may be nearby, hoping to catch another penguin meal.*

▲ *This picture captures an emperor penguin "porpoising," or catching a quick breath as it leaps from the water. Dolphins and porpoises use this method of breathing at top speed, too. When they aren't in a hurry, penguins just float or swim slowly on the surface.*

adaptations to keep them warm. The most important is their covering of feathers, which overlap like the tiles on a roof to form a strong waterproof layer.

Penguins may look clumsy on land, but in the water they move with grace and speed. Their **streamlined** shape lets them move smoothly through the water. Their feet and stubby tail combine to form a rudder, helping them steer. Their flippers, powered by strong chest muscles, beat up and down, **propelling** them through the water.

All penguins have a white front and dark back, which acts as **camouflage** at sea. A **predator** looking down on a swimming penguin has difficulty seeing the dark shape against the dark water. From below, the penguin's white front is hard to see against lighter surface waters.

Of all the species of penguins, the emperor is by far the largest. Standing about 3 feet high, it weighs anywhere from 42 to 100 pounds. Emperor penguins can stay underwater for up to 18 minutes and dive over 1,500 feet down—far deeper than any other bird.

▲ *The fairy penguin, or blue penguin, is the smallest of all penguins.*

4
Baleen Whales

Whales, dolphins, and porpoises together make up a group of sea **mammals** called **cetaceans**. There are about eighty species of cetaceans. As scientists learn more about whales, they sometimes decide that the differences within one species are significant enough to constitute two or more additional species. New species are sometimes found, too. In fact, a new species of beaked whale was discovered just as this book was being written.

There are two types of cetaceans: toothed whales and baleen whales. Baleen whales have rows of baleen, or

A humpback whale mother and calf swim near the surface. Like most baleen whales, humpback whales spend several months each year migrating between breeding grounds in warm waters and feeding grounds in cold seas. ▶

▲ *A right whale calf swims over to have a good look.*

"whalebone," hanging from the roof of their mouth, like the teeth of a comb. The baleen acts like a sieve, or strainer, that traps krill or small fish caught in the whale's mouth.

Most baleen whales migrate long distances each year. They spend their summers at feeding grounds in Arctic seas and around Antarctica. There they feed in the cold, plankton-rich seas, building up their food reserves as fat, or blubber, which will keep them alive through a winter in **tropical seas**, where there is little or no food. While traveling and at their breeding grounds in warm seas, adult whales normally do not eat; instead, they use the food reserves stored in their blubber.

Baleen whales include: the blue whale, the heaviest animal ever to live on Earth; the humpback whale, also known as the singing whale; and the right whale. The right whale was so called because it was the "right" whale to catch. It swam slowly, it was often found near the shore, it floated to the surface when it was killed, and it yielded large amounts of oil and whalebone. Right whales were the first whale species to be commercially hunted in the 1600s. By 1850, they were hunted nearly to extinction, and the species has never fully recovered. Even today there are fewer than 10,000 right whales in the world.

5
Toothed Whales

Toothed whales are hunters with sharp teeth that they use to catch and hold their **prey**, which they normally swallow whole. Sperm whales, pilot whales, orcas, beaked whales, beluga whales, **narwhals**, and all species of dolphins and porpoises are toothed whales.

The sperm whale is not only the biggest of the toothed whales, but also the largest toothed predator the world has ever seen! The largest of the meat-eating dinosaurs grew to a length of forty-five feet and weighed up to eight tons. The sperm whale grows to sixty-five feet in length and weighs a massive sixty tons. Its brain, which weighs twenty pounds, is the largest brain of any animal on

This orca is toying with a blue shark, the way a cat plays with a live mouse or bird it has caught. ▶

▲ An orca carries around a stingray before eating it. Orcas are fearsome predators—*fast, fierce, and highly intelligent. Luckily, they don't eat photographers! In fact, there is no known case of an orca killing a human in the wild. It's a remarkable record, one that is much, much better than the record of human behavior toward orcas!*

Earth. The sperm whale can dive as deep as two miles, and its dives can last over two hours.

Although they are called whales, orcas and pilot whales really belong to the dolphin group of cetaceans. Orcas, or killer whales, have the most varied **diet** of all whales. They **prey** on at least twenty species of whales and dolphins and also eat seals, sea lions, penguins, sharks, fish, squid, seabirds, turtles, and much, much more.

A sperm whale lifts its fluke high, starting a deep dive that can last over two hours. Sperm whales roam all of the world's oceans, except the polar seas. They are by far the largest of all the toothed whales. ▶

6

Dolphins and Porpoises

Dolphins are found in seas worldwide, except the very coldest. Orcas, largest of the dolphins, are an exception. Some dolphins, such as the common and bottlenose dolphins, are found all over the world; others live along a stretch of coastline or in a particular river. Some, such as Fraser's dolphins, are found only in warm waters, while others, such as right whale dolphins, live only in cool waters.

▲ *Dusky dolphins frolic underwater.*

There are at least thirty-three species of oceanic dolphins, depending on whom you ask. For example, there are many differences among bottlenose dolphins around the world, and some scientists believe there are really two or three different species, not just one.

Dolphins have sharp, pointed teeth for catching and holding their prey, which they usually swallow whole and headfirst. Their teeth are all the same size and shape. Many dolphins have a beak, or snout. Dolphins love to play with other dolphins, with whales, and even with people. They surf on waves, jump and chase, invent games, play with fish or seaweed, and speed alongside boats.

Porpoises differ from dolphins: none of the six species of porpoises are playful, and they usually avoid people. They are smaller than most dolphins, and stouter. Their rounded head has no beak. Their teeth are spade-shaped, for cutting up fish too big to be swallowed whole.

The five species of river dolphins are unique in that they are adapted to life in murky water where their vision is obscured. Most river dolphins are highly endangered, and one—the Yangtze River dolphin—will probably be **extinct** soon.

Dolphins and porpoises are hunters, preying on many kinds of squid and fish, especially small schooling fish such as sardines and herrings. They often work together in groups to capture their prey.

7
Seals and Sea Lions

Seals and sea lions are among the mammals that have adapted to a life at sea. Unlike whales and dolphins, they rest, **molt**, and give birth on beaches or sea ice. Like all other mammals, they are warm-blooded, they breathe air to stay alive, and they give birth to live young that **suckle** in order to **survive**.

▲ *For hours these fur seal pups have been playing in shallow pools on the rocky shoreline. This is good practice for their first swim in the open sea.*

Seals are found in many of the world's seas, and in a few lakes, too; however, most seals live in colder waters in the southern and northern hemispheres. They range in size from the 110-pound ringed seal of the Arctic to the elephant seal, which can grow to be twenty feet long and weigh as much as four tons.

There are two main kinds of seals: those with ears and those without ears, or true seals. Eared seals can turn their back flippers forward and walk, or at least waddle, on land and ice. Some can run faster than a human. In fact, I've met some of those! Sea lions and fur seals are eared seals. True seals move on land or ice by wriggling like a caterpillar, or slithering from side to side like a snake.

NOTES

Southern elephant seals are amazing! They spend most of the year at sea in the cold waters around Antarctica. They dive almost nonstop, day and night. A normal dive lasts twenty to thirty minutes and can reach depths of 2,000 feet. Each dive is followed by two to three minutes on the surface. Then the seals go back down again, searching for yet more fish and squid. A big dive by a large elephant seal lasts for two hours and reaches depths of 6,500 feet!

▼ *This fur seal is pictured with a recent catch.*

8
Fish

There are over 20,000 species of fish living in the sea. The smallest fish are very, very small. Over 10,000 of these species weigh less than an ounce. Others grow to be very large. The largest of all is the whale shark, a gentle giant that lives in tropical seas. The largest measured whale shark was forty-one feet long, but they may grow to be sixty feet long.

▲ *Sunfish like this one are the tallest fish in the world. They can measure up to fourteen feet from top to bottom and ten feet in length. These slow-moving fish can weigh over two tons.*

Many fish swim in groups called shoals or **schools**. A school is a group of fish of the same size and species all moving together in the same direction, and all changing direction at the same time.

▲ *These golden trevally are swimming in the open ocean.*

There are many good reasons for fish to form schools. Predators find it hard to pick out a single fish when they all look exactly the same and are all darting around in the water. Schooling makes swimming easier for most of the fish in the school. And finding food or a mate is easier, too.

NOTES

A large school of mackerel swims up against the sunlight in clear seas. Diving in schools like this is like watching an underwater dance: always changing, and always beautiful.

9

Fast Fish

Speed is the key to survival for many fish. Speed helps them catch fast-moving prey and avoid becoming the prey of larger, faster predators. Other ways of not getting eaten include being poisonous, being too prickly, having spines that get caught in a predator's mouth, and being too hard, like the turtle with its tough shell and skin.

But for many fish, speed is often the best option—or speed combined with schooling behavior.

▼ *Mahimahi*

NOTES

When flying fish are being chased by predators, they shoot out of the water at high speed and then glide above the sea's surface on their wing-like fins, sometimes over long distances.

▲ Blue sharks like this one are named for their deep blue color. They are predators of the open ocean, preying mostly on fish.

This sailfish, the sea's speed champion, is in cruising mode. ▶

When thousands of fish are swimming in a tight school, predators find it hard to pick out a single fish.

There are many speedsters in the sea, all of them hunters of squid or other fast fish. And sometimes they themselves become hunted. Some of the fastest fish are marlin, tuna, swordfish, wahoo, mako sharks, and blue sharks. But fastest of all is the sailfish, which has been timed at over sixty-eight miles per hour—even faster than a cheetah on land!

10
The Drifters

Plankton are the sea's drifters—the plants and animals that float freely in the water. They cannot swim, or they are weak swimmers, so they drift at the mercy of the currents, tides, and storms.

Most plankton are small. Large plankton include jellyfish, **salpas**, sea gooseberries, and krill. Krill are shrimp-like animals that often live in huge schools. They are the main source of food for most large whales and many other large animals.

The most important plankton are the plant plankton, or **phytoplankton**. These are plants so tiny that a million of them can fit into a

◂ *Jellyfish are weak swimmers and so, like all other kinds of plankton, they drift wherever the ocean currents take them.*

Small fish are using this large, colorful jellyfish as shelter. ▸

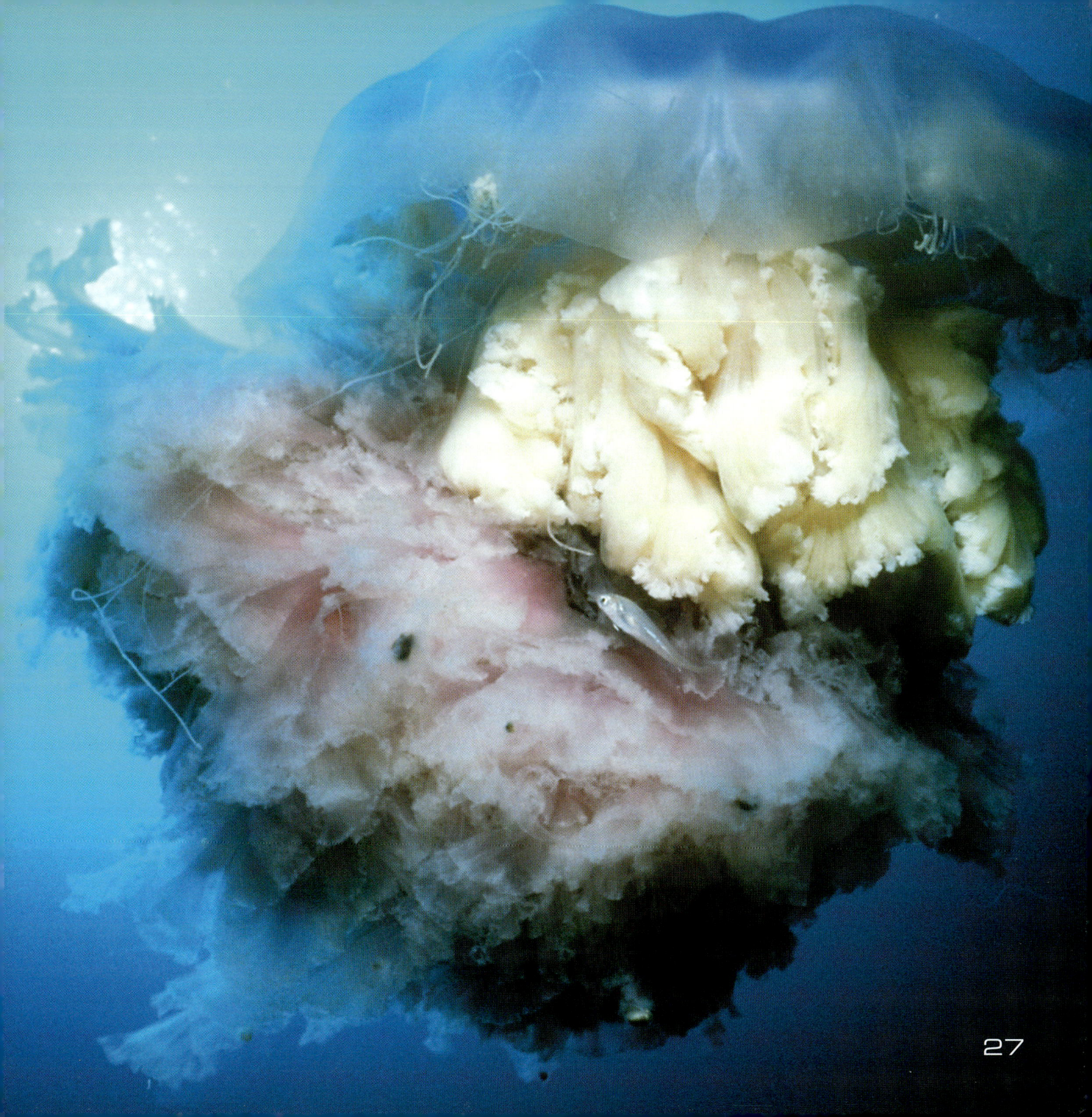

A swarm of krill swims through a giant kelp forest. Antarctic krill are among the most abundant animals on the planet. There can be up to a million of them in a cubic yard of seawater. ▶

teaspoon of seawater. They use sunlight and minerals from the water to make food. We could call these tiny plants "the grass of the sea," because they are the beginning of the sea's food chain, the way grass often is on land. Small animals eat the tiny plant plankton and become a source of food for larger animals. Phytoplankton produces *more than half* of the world's oxygen through a process called **photosynthesis**. Scientists believe that 90 percent of all photosynthesis takes place in the world's oceans. Trees, grasses, and other plants on land produce the rest.

11
Turtles and Squid

Jellyfish are the favorite food of another ocean traveler, the leatherback turtle. The leatherback is not only the largest sea turtle, but also the Earth's largest living reptile. It grows to nine feet in length and weighs nearly one ton. Leatherback turtles are found in all the world's oceans. They are superb divers that can reach depths of 3,000 feet or more in search of food. All turtles are good swimmers; the leatherback is one of the fastest, speeding along at up to twenty miles per hour.

▲ *The leatherback turtle is the largest reptile on Earth.*

Squid are fast, intelligent predators, feeding mostly on fish and krill.

Squid are fast, too, sometimes shooting out of the sea so fast that they can land on a boat deck twelve feet above the sea's surface. They are smart, fast hunters, often following the schools of krill or fish they feed on. They are found in all the world's oceans, often in large numbers. Squid range from tiny to huge: most are well under six feet long, but a few species are bigger.

The biggest of all squid are the giant squid that live in deep oceans around the world. They are best known for their fights with sperm whales, a fight the whale nearly always wins. Scientists now say that the giant squid's maximum size is 37 feet long with a weight of 550 pounds, though there are many stories of them growing much larger.

▲ *Like the leatherback, this green turtle can swim at speeds of up to twenty miles per hour.*

Glossary

Antarctica: An uninhabited continent surrounding the South Pole

Arctic: The cold, barren region surrounding the North Pole

Camouflage: A device used by some animals to blend into their surroundings in order to avoid being seen by predators or prey

Cetaceans: Large aquatic mammals that have a streamlined body; a group of mammals made up of dolphins, porpoises, and whales

Diet: The food that an animal or a person usually eats

Extinct: To gradually disappear due to diminishing numbers

Habitat: A place where animals and plants live and grow

Krill: A very small shrimp-like marine animal that is a primary source of food for penguins, whales, and many other inhabitants of Antarctica

Mammals: A class of warm-blooded animals in which the female feeds the young with its own milk

Migrate: To move from one region or habitat to another in response to regular seasonal changes

Molt: To periodically shed feathers, hair, or skin and replace what is lost with new growth

Narwhals: Small Arctic whales with spotted bodies, short flippers, and, in the male, a long ivory tusk

Penguins: Flightless, web-footed seabirds that use their flipper-shaped wings for swimming

Photosynthesis: A process by which plants or plantlike organisms use sunlight to make food/energy

Phytoplankton: Tiny, free-floating algae that live near the surface of seas worldwide

Predator: An animal that hunts, catches, and eats other animals

Prey (n): Animals that are hunted and eaten by other animals

Prey (v): To stalk, or hunt, an animal or group of animals

Propel: To move something forward

Salpas: Tiny marine organisms with transparent, barrel-shaped bodies

Schools: Groups of marine animals of a single type

Species: Types of animals that have some physical characteristics in common

Streamlined: Designed to move very quickly and gracefully

Suckle: To drink a mother's milk; to nurse

Survive: To stay alive and thrive

Tropical Seas: Bodies of water that are very warm throughout the year

Tubenoses: Seabirds with tube-shaped nostrils on the top of their beaks